GIRLS ROCK!
Contents

Carly *Mai*

CHAPTER 1

Big Day Out

Carly's parents have invited Mai to join them for a weekend on the Gold Coast. They're off to Rock 'n' Ride World—one of the biggest and best theme parks in the world.

Carly "Hey, Mai, have you seen this brochure? Look how many rides there are!"

Mai "Wow! We won't have enough time to go on them all. We'll need two weekends, not one."

Carly "You're right. Remember when we went to Ocean World last year and I swam with the dolphins?"

Mai "Yes, and we watched that brilliant IMAX film about whales and we all got sprayed with water."

Carly "I think Rock 'n' Roll World will be even better than that."

Mai "Yes, it'll be so cool."

Carly "I don't know how I'll sleep tonight. I'll probably dream I'm on the most amazing roller coaster that takes me way up into space!"

Mai "Now you're really getting carried away."

Carly "There's just so many to choose from. I want to go on the Pirate Roller. It looks like it swings right around."

Mai "Yes, and look at the Blender! It's meant to be the scariest ride there."

Carly "I can't wait for tomorrow!"

CHAPTER 2

Rides Galore

It's Saturday morning at Rock 'n' Ride World. Carly's parents arrange to meet the girls for lunch. They all head off.

Carly "Isn't it good our brothers didn't come! I wouldn't want to hang out with them. They'd be far too scared of the rides we want to go on."

Mai "Yes, they're real scaredy-cats.
Hey look, what's that big tower?"

Mai points at a huge ride. It seems
so high that the top of the ride is
nearly disappearing into the clouds.

Carly "That's the Tall Fall. You go up the pole, then free-fall to the bottom."

Mai "How scary! Let's do it!"

The girls are soon fastened into their seats.

Carly "I bet I don't scream the whole way down."

Mai "Yes right! You screamed diving off the high tower at the swimming pool. There's no way that you won't scream on this ride."

Carly "Here we go!"

Carly and Mai "Aarraaaggghhh!"

When the ride finally stops, Carly and Mai stagger off.

Carly "I wasn't scared at all but you were. Everyone at the park could hear you scream."

Mai "What about you? You sounded like a fire engine with its siren on."

Carly "Here's the Pirate Roller. Are you up for it?"

Mai "Definitely. It looks brilliant!"

The girls have two turns then head off to try their luck at the side stalls.

Carly "There they are. I love the clowns. I want to win a soft toy."

Mai "Cool. Let's go over."

The girls decide to get three balls each to throw in the clown's mouth.

Carly "Ready? Here goes."

Carly and Mai use all their balls but they don't have any luck.

Mai "Come on. Let's go through the spinning barrel."

Carly "But I'm hopeless at staying up."

Mai "So am I. That's the whole idea!"

Carly and Mai weave their way through the barrel, laughing and falling on top of each other as they go.

After the barrels, the girls walk
past some funny mirrors.

Carly "Look! You've turned into
Miss Longhead."
Mai "And you're seriously twisted in
the middle!"
Carly "Let's swap. Now I'll be Miss
Longhead."
Mai "And I'll get twisted!"

CHAPTER 3
Full of Food

It's lunchtime and the girls have met up with Carly's parents as arranged.

Carly "These hot dogs are really good."

Mai "I thought you must have liked them ... you've eaten four!"

Carly "How many hot dogs have you ever eaten in one go?"

Mai "I'm not sure, but I know it's not as many as you."

After lunch, the girls say goodbye to Carly's parents and go in search of more rides.

Mai "What's next? Ready to be really scared yet?"

Carly "Not quite. I'm still hungry."

Mai (pointing) "There's an ice cream van. Do you want to go halves on an ice cream?"

Carly "Halves? No way! I want my own."

Mai "You sure that's a good idea? Don't forget we've still got the Blender to go."

Carly "I've never been sick in my life from a ride. There's not one that could make me puke!"

The girls buy their ice creams.
Carly decides on a double cornet and
Mai gets a single.

Carly "I shouldn't have eaten mine
    so fast. I've got a brain freeze."
Mai "I think you already had a brain
    freeze. Come on, there's the Blender!"
Carly "Look how fast it goes!"
Mai "And how high!"

CHAPTER 4

Stir It Up

The Blender is the scariest ride at
Rock 'n' Ride World. Carly and Mai
race to their seats as soon as their
turn comes.

Carly "I've done up my belt, only it's
really tight."

Mai "At least you know you won't fall out."

Carly "I hope my ice cream doesn't turn to mush in the Blender. Maybe eating a double cornet before this ride wasn't such a good move."

Mai "Well, I just hope your double cornet stays inside your stomach."

The ride starts. The Blender turns
upside down and spins around
and around. The girls scream.
Aaahhhhhhh!

Mai "That was amazing!"
Carly "Yes, totally!"

Carly "How about when we turned
360 degrees in our seats? It felt like
my head was going to drop off."

Mai "Yes, and my stomach is still
spinning. Let's go again ... right
now!"

The girls have three more turns on
the Blender.

Carly "I don't know how many more times I can do this. My stomach feels like it's full of butterflies."

Mai "I told you not to pig out on all that ice cream. It might be time to give it a rest before we're really sorry. You know, what goes down must come up."

Carly "Yes, maybe you're right.
Ice cream doesn't mix so well with
hot dogs and tomato sauce."

Mai "Well, we'll find a calmer ride
next. My stomach needs a rest, too!"

Carly (pointing) "Let's sit down over
there for a minute. Come on."

CHAPTER 5

Look Out Below!

After a quick rest, the girls head off again. They buy some popcorn along the way.

Mai "I'd love to own a theme park like Rock 'n' Ride World."
Carly "Yes, then you could have your own rules."

Mai "I'd ban all boys."

Carly "Absolutely."

Mai "I wouldn't want their smelly germs in my park and besides, they'd eat all the food."

Carly "Not if I got to it first."

Mai "True!"

Both girls giggle as they continue walking around.

Carly "Let's go on the Ferris wheel."

Mai "OK, cool. It's meant to be the biggest in the world."

Carly "What'll we do with our popcorn?"

Mai "Take it with us. Ferris wheels go really slow."

Mai and Carly find a seat on the
Ferris wheel and take the popcorn
with them. Soon they are sitting at
the top overlooking the crowd below.

Mai "Wow! We're so high, I can see
the whole world from up here."

Carly "Everyone looks like ants."

Mai "Why aren't we moving? This thing's taking forever to get going."

A few minutes pass and the girls are still in the same spot.

Carly "I think it's broken down. Maybe we'll have to climb out of here and abseil down to the bottom."

Mai "Yes, like Spiderman, I mean
Spiderwoman."

Carly "Or Lara Croft from *Tomb
Raider*."

A few more minutes pass and the
Ferris wheel still hasn't moved.

Mai "This is boring. We've been here
for ages. Let's see how many people
we can hit with our popcorn."

Carly "Great. Get ready, now aim! Take that!"

The girls throw pieces of popcorn at the people walking below.

Mai "Everyone keeps looking up but they don't know it's us."
Carly "It's like it's raining popcorn. That would be so cool!"

The Ferris wheel starts to move again, taking the girls back towards the ground.

Mai (looking below) "Hey, look at those security guards standing down there."
Carly "I think they've got a handful of popcorn."
Mai "Uh-oh!"

The Ferris wheel stops at the bottom. Mai and Carly get off. The security guards glare at the girls.

Mai "Excuse me. I think that's our popcorn. It sort of fell over the edge when we were stuck up there."
Carly "Yes, sorry about that."

The security guards tell the girls they shouldn't have taken food on to the Ferris wheel in the first place.

Carly "We'd better go. Mum and Dad will be waiting."

Mai "I've had the best time. My favourite ride was the Blender."

Carly "Yes, it really was amazing."

Mai "Next time we should take some milk and ice cream on with us and make instant milk shakes!"

Carly "Yes, as long as the security guards don't see!"

Theme Park Lingo

Mai

Carly

adrenaline A natural substance in your body that kicks in when you react to an exciting or scary challenge.

dizzy attack What happens when you shut your eyes on a fast moving ride, then get off and try to stand still.

free-fall What you do on a ride that falls really quickly from a great height. It's an amazing feeling but really scary!

G force This is the force you feel when you speed up or slow down really, really quickly, like when you're on a fast ride.

sick ride A really cool ride—not a ride that makes you sick!

GIRLS ROCK!
Theme Park Must-dos

☆ Don't put anything in your pockets that might fly out when you're on a ride.

☆ Make sure that you go on all the rides, especially the really scary ones.

☆ Don't eat too much food before you go on a ride, or you might be sorry.

☆ Make sure that you are strapped into your seat properly before the ride starts.

☆ Take a pair of earplugs on to the ride in case you are sitting beside someone who screams.

☆ Take your hat off before you go on a ride.

☆ Take lots of friends with you when you go to your favourite theme park. You're sure to have lots of fun!

GIRLS ROCK!
Theme Park Instant Info

 Theme parks are very popular places for families. Two favourites in Britain are Alton Towers and Thorpe Park.

 The biggest theme park in the world is Disneyland in the United States. Disneyland was named after its creator Walt Disney.

 The greatest number of roller coasters ridden in a 24-hour period is 74.

 Four friends in the USA rode roller coasters in ten parks across four states in record time. They used helicopters to travel between them.

The United States is the country with the most number of theme and amusement parks in the world.

 The biggest Ferris wheel in the world is the Dai-Kanransha big wheel at Palette Town grounds in Tokyo, Japan. The Ferris wheel is 115 metres high and can carry 384 passengers.

 The world-famous kids' group, The Wiggles, have a themed area called Wiggles World at Australia's Dreamworld.

GIRLS ROCK!
Think Tank

1 What are two favourite theme parks in Britain?

2 Why should you take earplugs to a theme park?

3 What is the most roller coasters ridden in one day?

4 Who would you see wherever you go at Wiggles World?

5 In what country is the world's biggest Ferris wheel?

6 What substance in your body kicks in when you are about to do something really exciting or scary?

7 What direction are you heading in when you free-fall?

8 Which theme park is the largest in the world?

Answers

1 Two favourite theme parks in Australia are Alton Towers and Thorpe Park.

2 You should take earplugs in case you sit next to someone on a ride who screams.

3 The most roller coasters ridden in one day is 74.

4 You would see The Wiggles—mostly pictures of them, not the real thing, of course!

5 The world's biggest Ferris wheel is in Japan.

6 Adrenaline kicks in when you feel excited or scared.

7 You are heading straight down when you free-fall!

8 Disneyland is the largest theme park in the world.

How did you score?

- If you got all 8 answers correct, you should run your own theme park one day!

- If you got 6 answers correct, head straight for the Ferris wheel when you go to a theme park—your stomach will thank you.

- If you got fewer than 4 answers correct, then stick to the local park.

Hey Girls!

I hope that you have as much fun reading my story as I have had writing it. I loved reading and writing stories when I was young.

At school, why don't you use "Wild Ride" as a play and you and your friends can be the actors.

Create some rides from furniture and blankets. You and your friends could mime to show the motion of the rides. Maybe you could make some popcorn, too.

So ... have you decided who is going to be Mai and who is going to be Carly? Now, with your friends, read and act out this play in front of your classmates. It'll definitely make the whole class laugh.

You can also take the story home and get someone to act out the parts with you.

So, get ready to have more fun with your reading than the Easter Bunny at Easter!

And remember, Girls Rock!

Shey Kettle.

GIRLS ROCK!
When We Were Kids

Shey *Jacqueline*

Shey talked to Jacqueline, another *Girls Rock!* author.

Shey "Did you ever go to a theme park when you were little?"

Jacqueline "Yeah, I went to Luna Park."

Shey "Were you scared?"

Jacqueline "No, not at all."

Shey "But what about the rides?"

Jacqueline "I loved them all, especially the ones that went round and round and round."

Shey "Wow! You were brave."

Jacqueline "Not really. They all looked great from my pram!"

GIRLS ROCK!
What a Laugh!

Q What is the best thing to eat on a roller coaster?

A I scream!

GIRLS ROCK!

The Sleepover

Pool Pals

Bowling Buddies

Girl Pirates

Netball Showdown

School Play Stars

Diary Disaster

Horsing Around

Newspaper Scoop

Snowball Attack

Dog on the Loose

Escalator Escapade

Cooking Catastrophe

Talent Quest

Wild Ride

Camping Chaos

Mummy Mania

Skater Chicks

GIRLS ROCK! books are available from most booksellers. For mail order information please call Rising Stars on 0870 40 20 40 8 or visit www.risingstars-uk.com

44